Clarion Books
a Houghton Mifflin Company imprint
215 Park Avenue South, New York, NY 10003

Text copyright © 2006 by Carl Norac
Illustrations copyright © 2006 by Ingrid Godon
Published by arrangement with Macmillan Children's Books,
a division of Macmillan Publishers Ltd., United Kingdom.
First American edition, 2007.

The illustrations were executed in paint and pastels on textured paper.
The text was set in 35-point Pastonchi.

www.clarionbooks.com

Printed in Belgium.

Library of Congress Cataloging-in-Publication Data

Norac, Carl.
[My mummy is magic]
My mommy is magic / by Carl Norac ; illustrated by Ingrid Godon. — 1st American ed.
p. cm.
First published in the United Kingdom in 2006 by Macmillan Children's Books
under the title My mummy is magic.
Summary: A child lists things a mommy does, such as chasing monsters away,
that show she is magic, even if she does not have a wand or magic hat.
ISBN-13: 978-0-618-75766-4
ISBN-10: 0-618-75766-X
[1. Mother and child—Fiction. 2. Magic—Fiction.] I. Godon, Ingrid, ill. II. Title.
PZ7.N775115My5 2007
[E]—dc22
2006007149

10 9 8 7 6 5 4 3 2 1

My Mommy Is
MAGIC

by Carl Norac
Illustrated by Ingrid Godon

CLARION BOOKS · NEW YORK

My mommy doesn't
have a magic hat or
a wand. She doesn't
need things like that.
She's just magic.

When I have
nightmares, my
mommy chases
the monsters away.

9

When I whisper a secret
in my mommy's ear,
she guesses it before
I finish telling her!

If I hurt myself,
my mommy kisses
the sore place,
and . . . *Ta-da!*
It's all better.

When my mommy swims
with me, we go faster
than the dolphins.

My mommy's favorite dress
is blue with little clouds on it.
When she wears it, the sky
is always clear.

When my mommy plants
seeds, flowers always grow.

When my mommy sings,
butterflies come to listen.

Sometimes I'm magic too.
When I sing and dance,
I always make my mommy laugh.

My mommy can make things
appear. For my birthday, she
made a cake as big as a rocket!

And she can make things disappear. When my mommy tells me stories, everything else falls away. There's only the two of us, traveling through time and space.

My mommy is magic,
and when I grow up,

I'm going to be
magic too.